Chi's
Sweet Adventures

④

Created by Konami Kanata
Adapted by Kinoko Natsume

VERTICAL
COMICS

Chi's Sweet Adventures ④

Chi
A 2~3 month-old female gray Tabby kitten. She's small, but brimming with curiosity and energy!

Yohei
The Yamadas' son, a second grader. Chi calls him Yohey. He's honest and thoughtful.

Daddy
Mr. Yamada. Because he's a designer, he often works at home.

Mommy
Mrs. Yamada. She's kind and good at cooking. Sometimes she's a little too carefree.

Blackie
He looks scary, but he's actually soft-hearted. He teaches Chi how to be a cat. He's the boss of Chi's neighborhood.

Cocchi
A stray kitten who lives in a cardboard box at the park. He's a bit of a braggart, but is actually very nice and kind of shy.

Ann
Chi and Cocchi's new kitten friend. She's always with her big brother, Terry. She's sweet and down to earth.

Terry
Ann's brother and friend to Chi and Cocchi. He can be a little indecisive, but you can rely on him when push comes to shove.

Chi's Sweet Adventures ④

Chi is Delighted, Part 1

5

Continued in Part 2

6

Continued in Part 3

Chi is Delighted, Part 3

Continued in Part 4

Chi is Delighted, Part 4

Continued in Part 5

Chi is Delighted, Part 5

Continued in Part 6

Chi is Delighted, Part 6

Continued in Part 7

The end

Chi Runs Away, Part 1

12

Continued in Part 2

Chi Runs Away, Part 2

Continued in Part 3

Chi Runs Away, Part 3

Continued in Part 4

Continued in Part 5

N-NOW WHAT SHOULD CHI DO~?

NYAA?

NYAA?

NYAAN?

SO TIWED...

AUNTY WILL TAKE GOOD CARE OF THAT FISH FOR YOU.

CREEP

CREEP

NYAA?

EEK?!

YOU! OVER HERE!

NYA!

OH! THAT SOUNDS LIKE...

!!!

CHI!!

MRAR!!

ZHFF ZHFF

AUNTY CALICO!

MYA!

NYA?

LOOKS LIKE YOU'VE BEEN THROUGH A LOT.

DON'T LET HER TRICK YOU! RUN!!

MYA?!

HUH?!

BUT EVERYTHING'S GOING TO BE ALL RIGHT NOW.

GLEEAAM

NYAAAN?

HUH?!

WHAT'S HAPPENING?!

16

Continued in Part 6

Chi Runs Away, Part 6

17

Continued in Part 7

Chi Runs Away, Part 7

18

The end

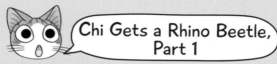

Chi Gets a Rhino Beetle, Part 1

FLUTTR
FLUTTR

WHERE'D IT GO?

MYA?

WAAIIT!

MYAAH!

SCURRY

HEH HEH, LOOKS LIKE CHI'S HAVING FUN.

??

FLIT FLIT

WAIT! WAIT!

MYAA!!

WHY DON'T YOU JOIN IN, YOHEI?

HUH?

FWITT

LET'S GO BUG HUNTING!

YAY!

19

Continued in Part 2

Chi Gets a Rhino Beetle, Part 2

20

Continued in Part 3

Chi Gets a Rhino Beetle, Part 3

21

Continued in Part 4

Chi Gets a Rhino Beetle, Part 4

CICADAS CAN SEE WHAT'S BEHIND THEM, BUT THEY CAN'T REALLY SEE THE TREE THEY'RE ON, SO...

CICADAS ARE ON ALERT WHEN THEY'RE SILENT. SNAG THEM WHILE THEY'RE LOUD!!

OKAY!!

YOU GRAB THEM FROM BEHIND THE TREE LIKE THIS!!

SNATCH

I DID IT! I GOT ONE!

I'M GONNA GET MORE~!

WOW!!

EH HEM.

...UH.

HMM... HOW SHOULD I GET THIS ONE?

WAH! HELP!

MREEN MRE MRE!!

AH HA HA HA.

MYAH!!

22

Continued in Part 5

Chi Gets a Rhino Beetle, Part 5

HEE HEE.

YOU SURE GOT A LOT!

HEH HEH HEH, WE'RE GONNA MAKE IT TOGETHER.

?

YEAH... BUT I'M A LITTLE BUMMED WE DIDN'T GET A RHINO BEETLE.

MYA?

IT'S A BEETLE TRAP!!

HEY!

LIKE THIS?

LOOKS GREAT!

I BROUGHT THE THING YOU ASKED FOR.

WHAT IS THIS?

LET'S COME BACK AT NIGHT TO CHECK IT.

OKAY!!

23

Continued in Part 6

Chis Gets a Rhino Beetle, Part 6

HUH...? NOTH-ING...

I WONDER IF THERE'LL BE A BEETLE.

HOW ABOUT THE NEXT TREE?

MYA?

BANANAS ARE RHINO BEETLE'S FAVORITE, SO THEY'LL COME TO EAT IT!

Banana Trap

Mash a banana

Put it in the net

Hang it on a tree

WASSAT?

MYA~?

YEAH! YOU'RE RIGHT!!

NOW LET'S GO CHECK IT!

MYAA~♡

IT SMELLS GOOD~!

Continued in Part 7

THERE WEREN'T BEETLES ON ANY OF THE TREES...

SLUMP

MYAAA!!

WHAAAT!!

IT'S A RHINO BEETLE!

CHI, WHAT'S WRONG...? OH!

MYA?

YUM~!

HEY! THAT'S THE BANANA TRAP!!

HEH HEH.

RSTL

RSTL

YOHEY!

C'MON, CHI! THIS IS FOR THE BEETLES!

MYA!

IT'S ALL THANKS TO YOU, CHI! THANK YOU!!

MYA!!

MYA

PWOP

HM?

AREN'T YOU GLAD YOU GOT A BEETLE?

CHI BRINGS IN THE BEETLES!

25

The end

Chi Plays Around, Part 1

Continued in Part 2

Chi Plays Around, Part 2

MYA MYA

LET'S PLAY!

MYAA~!

...

YOHEI, DIDN'T WE PLAY LIKE THIS A LOT WHEN YOU WERE YOUNGER?

YOHEI!

MYA?

HUH?

I FOUND SOMETHING NEAT~

WASSAT?

MYA?

THIS IS FUN!!

MYAA~!!

LOOK, DOESN'T IT BRING BACK MEMORIES?

SURE...

CHI, WILL YOU PLAY WITH ME?!

MYAA♪

27

Continued in Part 3

Chi Plays Around, Part 3

28

Continued in Part 4

Chi Plays Around, Part 4

Continued in Part 5

Continued in Part 6

Chi Plays Around, Part 6

31

Continued in Part 7

Chi Plays Around, Part 7

I'M HOME! OH, THOSE TAKE ME BACK. I WANT TO JOIN IN!

HEY, LET'S DO THAT THING.

OH?! THAT THING?!

FLOAT

FLOAT...

MYAA!!

YOHEI!

POP

POP

MYA?!

FWOOOOSH

IT'S A HULA-HOOP BUBBLE!

LOOK, IT'S A BUBBLE HOOP!!

OH!!

YAAAAY~!!

SO COOL~!!

MYAA~!!

32

The end

Chi Hisses, Part 1

Continued in Part 2

Chi Hisses, Part 2

YOU HISS TO INTIMIDATE YOUR OPPONENTS.

INTIMIDATE?

MYA?

THIS IS...

NRR NRR!!

HOW YOU HISS!!

MAKE YOURSELF LOOK BIG AND STRONG SO YOUR OPPONENT SHRINKS BACK.

NRR

WHOA~

ZZZ...

SNOOOO

!!

MAKE YOUR EYES FLASH SHARPLY...

FLASH!!

HMM...

MYA...!

HSSSSSS!!

MYAH?!

FWOOSH

AND FLOOF OUT YOUR BACK AND STICK OUT YOUR TAIL!

THAT WAS A SHOCK!

MYA?!

NRR!!

I'M SHOCKED YOU CAN FALL ASLEEP THAT FAST!

Continued in Part 3

Chi Hisses, Part 3

Continued in Part 4

Chi Hisses, Part 4

OKAY, TRY TO INTIMIDATE THEM.

CHIRP CHIRP

IT'S PWEY!

HISSS!

HISS!

JUMP

...

HUH?

MYA...?!

CHIRP

CHIRP

RIBBIT!

SPROING

WHOA?!

MYAAA?!

NRR

O-OKAY, LET'S KEEP GOING. HISS AT THAT FROG!

RIBBIT!

THIS IS HARD!

MYAA!

NRR...

YOU'VE GOT A LONG WAY TO GO...

Continued in Part 5

Chi Hisses, Part 5

38

Continued in Part 6

CHI COULDN'T HISS VERY WELL...

MYA...

NRR

DON'T GIVE UP, PRACTICE AND YOU'LL GET BETTER.

PANT PANT

WHOA!

NRAR!

BLACKIE!

YOU'RE RIGHT...

MYA...

BOOM

WUFF?!

WUFF!!

NOO~!!

CHI!! HISS! YOU CAN DO IT!

MRGH MRGH!

HSSSSS!!

SHOOF

WUFF WUFF!!

O..... OKAY! CHI WILL TRY!!

H...

MRGH?!

WUFF WUFF WUU–UFF!

WHUMP

HE WASN'T INTIMIDATED BY ME...?!

HOW'S THAT?!

HISS ♡

AH... IT'S NO USE...

NRR...

Continued in Part 7

AWOO ♡

LOVE!

HUH?!

BYE, KITTY!

SO CUTE~

SNIFF SNIFF

Let's go home.

CHI, LOOKS LIKE YOUR HISSES MAKE OTHERS FALL IN LOVE WITH YOU.

NRR.

MYAA!?

WERE THEY IN LOVE?

YEAH, TO THE POINT I WANT TO LEARN IT, TOO.

NRR~

IN LOVE?

MYA?

OH, IT'S A KITTY!

THEN THIS TIME CHI WILL GIVE YOU LESSONS!

MYA!!

NRR...

O-OH, YEAH, NEXT TIME.

HISS~♡

AWW!

AWW!

SO CUTE~!♡

HSSS♡

I'LL TRY IT LATER...

40

The end

Chi Goes to the Ocean, Part 1

CHI DOESN'T LIKE IT IN HERE.

MYA~~!!

POP

CHI, WE'RE ALMOST THERE.

CHI, WE'RE HERE!

OH, IT SMELLS LIKE THE OCEAN!

IT'S THE BEACH!!

MYA?!

HUH? WASSAT SMELL?

SNIFF SNIFF

WHOA!!

MYAA!!

Continued in Part 2

Chi Goes to the Ocean, Part 2

ZHAA... ZHA

HEWLP~!! MYAA~! ROOOAAAAR HUH?! CHI!!

WAIT~! MYAA~! SCAMPER

SAFE!! LIFT ZHAAA

HUH? IT WENT AWAY? HUUSSSH MYA?

YOHEY! MYA~? CHI, LET'S RUN AFTER THE WAVES TOGETHER!!

HM? MYA? ZMM ZHA ZHA ZHA...

HEE HEE, LOOKS LIKE FUN.

42

Continued in Part 3

Chi Goes to the Ocean, Part 3

Continued in Part 4

Chi Goes to the Ocean, Part 4

WHOA, THAT'S A BIG ROCK! CHI, DON'T WANDER TOO FAR.

DASH!!

MYAA!!

HEY, WAIT!!

CHI?!

MYA?!

SHFFL

SHFFL

SLIP

SWIP

CHI!! FOUND YOU!

COME OUT~!

MYAA~!!

SKRITCH SKRITCH

MYAA!!

BUT CHI WAS SO CLOSE!

MYAA~!

WHAT'S WRONG, CHI?

Continued in Part 5

OKAY, LET'S GO HOME.

YEAH,

Ah ha ha ha!

Myaa!

VROOOM

Isn't this yummy?

Myaa!

WASN'T TODAY FUN, CHI...?

MYA...

HEH HEH, THEY'RE BOTH SOUND ASLEEP.

Isn't it great?

Myaa!

LET'S GO AGAIN NEXT YEAR.

45

The end

Chi Cools Off, Part 1

46

Continued in Part 2

Chi Cools Off, Part 2

47

Continued in Part 3

Chi Cools Off, Part 3

ANN! TERRY! LET US JOIN, TOO!!

MYAA!!

MYA?

SURE!

OH! IT'S PWEY!

MREEEN MREE MREE

AHH, IT'S COOL...

MYA...

SLUMP

AAH...

IT'S A CICADA! I'LL BE THE ONE TO CATCH IT!

CHIT TER!!

SPAK

WHOA! IT PEED ON ME?!

MRAR?!

SZZL SZZL SZZL...

Mi... Mini...

HA HA, COCCHI, YOU'RE FUNNY!

YOU STINK!

HOT HOT HOT!

OH, THE SHADE IS GONE!

DAMN IT! I'LL GET IT ON YOU, TOO!

MRAR!

WAAH, RUN AWAY!

Continued in Part 4

Continued in Part 5

Continued in Part 6

Chi Cools Off, Part 6

Continued in Part 7

Chi Cools Off, Part 7

The end

Yohei's Picture Journal, Part 1

HMM, WHAT SHOULD I DRAW FOR MY PICTURE JOURNAL...

OH, RIGHT!

"CHI LIKES BEING BRUSHED..."

MYAA♪

"TODAY I'LL INTRODUCE CHI."

YOHEY?

MYA?

"BUT SHE LIKES MOM'S VACUUM EVEN MORE."

MYAA♡

ROOAAR

"CHI PLAYS A LOT.

MYAAA

SHE REALLY LOVES EATING FOOD."

"EVEN WHEN SHE GETS IN TROUBLE,

CHI!! AGAIN ~?!

MYA??

SHE'S AMAZING BECAUSE SHE NEVER GETS SAD."

"AND SHE SLEEPS A LOT."

Z Z Z

"I LIKE EVERYTHING ABOUT CHI, BUT MY FAVORITE PART ABOUT HER IS

MYAN♪

CUDDL

CUDDL

WHEN SHE SNUGGLES UP TO ME."

Continued in Part 2

Yohei's Picture Journal, Part 2

MYAA

"CHI RECENTLY GOT HER OWN LITTLE CAR..."

OH...

CHI'S GOING OUT!

MYAN!

HMM, SOMETHING'S MISSING...

COME TO THINK OF IT, WE DON'T KNOW WHAT CHI DOES OUTSIDE...

YOU'RE RIGHT.

YOHEI, WHAT'S UP?

...

OKAY!

I'M WRITING ABOUT CHI IN MY DIARY.

SHFF

I'M SHERLOCK YOHEI HOLMES!!

I'LL GO AND TAIL CHI... I MEAN, DR. WATSON!

Continued in Part 3

Yohei's Picture Journal, Part 3

MYAA! COCCHI! MRR YO.

OH, THERE'S CHI!! WAIT, WAIT! MYAA!!

HMM, IS THAT HER FRIEND?!

HUH?! MYA?! MRAR!!
SCURRY

WHO-EVER GETS TO THE PARK FIRST WINS! MRAR!! MYA!! OKAY!

AHA HA! IT'S ALL WIGGLY! MYAA!! WGGL WGGL MRGH! IT'S FUNNY~!

READY... MYAA!! THAT'S CHEATING!! DASH AAH! I NEED TO HURRY AFTER THEM!

MYAA! CHI'S AMAZING!!

56

Continued in Part 4

MREEN

MREEN!!

CHITTER CHITTER CHITTER

MYA?!

AH...

MRRGH!!

IT'S PREY!

LET'S GET IT!

MYAA!

MYAAA!

wHUMP

MRAR!

CHI!!

MYAMYA!

SPROING

MRRAAR!!

MRGH!

SERIOUSLY, YOU'RE A HANDFUL.

LICK

HEE HEE HEE

MYAA!

LICK

CHI CAN CLIMB TREES?!

...

57

Continued in Part 5

Yohei's Picture Journal, Part 5

THEY'RE GOING AFTER A SPARROW NOW!

CHIRP CHIRP

WHAT'RE YOU DOING? SO HELPLESS!

MRGH!

MYAAAA!

POUNCE

TWEET TWEET

THANKS COCCHI!

MYA!!

...

FWOOSH

MYAA?!

OH... SHE'S CUDDLING WITH THAT CAT...

MYAA!!

CHI'S GONNA TWY HARDER!

CUDDL

CUDDL

KEH!!

MRGH!!

YOU OKAY?!

MRRA?!

I SEE ...

I'M GLAD YOU'VE GOT A BEST FRIEND, CHI...

58

Continued in Part 6

Yohei's Picture Journal, Part 6

LOOKS LIKE CHI IS GOING HOME.

MYA?

I'M HOME...

WEL-COME BACK.

MYA!!

NOM

WELCOME HOME, YOHEY!

MYAA!

...? WHAT'S SHE GOING TO DO WITH THAT CICADA?

CHI HAS A PWESENT!

MYA!

HM?

SPLAT

CHI'S HOME!

MYAA!

I REALLY DIDN'T KNOW ANYTHING ABOUT CHI.

HUH...?!

THE CICADA?!

Continued in Part 7

Yohei's Picture Journal, Part 7

CHI, I CAN'T BELIEVE YOU BROUGHT A BUG HOME.

CAN'T HAVE YOU DOING THAT.

OH, I SEE.

WOW!!

THANK YOU, CHI!

SQUEEZ

HUH?!

MYA!!

CHI, I'LL TREASURE THIS!

CHITTER CHITTER CHITTER

HUH?!

CHI WAS DOING ALL THOSE THINGS

WAAAH!

MREEN MREEN

CHITTER CHITTER

MYAA?!

FOR ME!

"EVERYTHING CHI DOES IS AMAZING.

MYA~!

THAT'S WHY I LOVE CHI!"

The end

Chi and the Secret Place, Part 1

Continued in Part 2

Chi and the Secret Place, Part 2

GET READY TO GO!!

MRRGH!!

JUST A LIL' MORE ...!

zNIKK

MADE IT!

MRAR!

YOU DID IT, CHI!

MYA!

MYAAA!!

SCURRY SCURRY

SCURRY

WHOA!

MYA〜〜!!

MYA

HUP TWO, HUP TWO

MYA

MYAA〜〜!!

IT'S AMAZING!!

Continued in Part 3

Chi and the Secret Place, Part 3

63

Continued in Part 4

Chi and the Secret Place, Part 4

THIS PLACE IS NICE...

STREEEETCH

!!

HM?

WHOAAA!!

MYAAA!!

MYAA~!!

CHI'S GONNA GO HIGHER!

CHI, WHAT'RE YOU DOING?

MYA?

SHFF

RSTL

RSTL

SHOOFF

HOW DO WE GET UP THERE?

MYAA?

WHAAT?!

MYAA~?!

Continued in Part 5

Chi and the Secret Place, Part 5

HMM
...

...

GUESS THAT WOULDN'T WORK...

MYAAA

HAAA

MRR

HOP

I DON'T THINK WE COULD JUMP THERE.

...

STAAARE

WHAT IF WE RIDE A GIANT SPARROW?

MYAA!!

FLOAT FLOAT FLOAT...

HUH?!

MYAH?!

OR MAYBE A LOT OF NORMAL ONES COULD...

HUH?!

NO WAY!!

MYAA~?!

65

Continued in Part 6

Chi and the Secret Place, Part 6

66

Continued in Part 7

The end

Chi Follows Blackie, Part 1

TOE...

TIP

THAT WAS SCAWY! CHI DIDN'T NOTICE YOU AT ALL~!

MYA!

HEH HEH.

MRR

HEH HEH HEH ...

AIN'T MY TIP TOEING GREAT?

MRGH

MYA!

IT'S AWE- SOME! CHI WANTS TO TWY!

MYAA?

WONDER IF COCCHI'S AROUND.

OH, IT'S BLACKIE!

MRRAAR!!

WAH !!

MYA?!

HOW ABOUT WE TRY IT OUT ON HIM ?

HEE HEE HEE...

YEAH !!

68

Continued in Part 2

Chi Follows Blackie, Part 2

Continued in Part 3

Chi Follows Blackie, Part 3

70

Continued in Part 4

Chi Follows Blackie, Part 4

OKAY, MAYBE I'LL GO TO THAT SHOP SOON.

NRR

YOU'RE PLAYING WITH YOUR FRIEND?

OH, IT'S THE BEAR CAT.

GOOD KITTY!

KEH! STOP THAT.

MRGH...

GLANCE

HM?

OKAY, CHI'S GOING!

MYA!

HOP

AH.

CHI!!

MYAA!!

YOHEY!!

DON'T STAY OUT TOO LATE, OKAY?

Continued in Part 5

Chi Follows Blackie, Part 5

OH, THIS IS...

MRAR...

MRGH...

OH, WELCOME, BOSS.

MRRGH

HUH?! HE LEFT SOME!

MYA?!

MRAR!!

WE'RE GOING FOR IT, CHI!!

PLEASE ENJOY YOUR MEAL!

NRR

THIS IS TASTY!!

YUMMY!!

MRR...

I'M REAL HUNGRY...

YEAH...

GROWWL

GROWWW

72

Continued in Part 6

Chi Follows Blackie, Part 6

WHERE'D HE GO?

WHEE!

MYA!!

CATCH

MRAR?

CHI'S IN HERE~!

HUH ...?

MYAA~!

HOP

HOP

MYA??

MRARRI!

YOU'VE DONE IT NOW!! GET BACK HERE!!

NO WAY!!

MYAA~!

SKEDADDLE

MYAAAA!!

CHI CAN'T GET OUT! HEWLP, COCCHI~!

BOING

Burnable Trash

RATTL

RATTL

MRRGH!!

CHI, JUST HOLD ON!!

SPROING

THIS SEEMS LIKE A GOOD PWACE.

MYA!

Burnable Trash

WHUNK

MRGH?!

MRRAA?

? WHERE'D YOU GO?!

Burnable Trash

MRRAAGH?!

OH NO!!

RATTL

RATTL

Burnable Trash

MYAA~~!!

73

Continued in Part 7

Chi Follows Blackie, Part 7

MYAAA...?

YOHEY... DADDY, MOMMY...

STOP THAT!

KLONK

WELL, I'M STARVED. SEE YA!

MRAR

SURE.

MYAA~!!

BLACKIE!

FOUND YA.

NRR

CHI, WE'RE HERE.

HUH? BLACKIE?

THANKS BLACKIE... ZZZ...

MYA...

NRR

IT'S LATE. GET YOURSELF HOME.

MYAA!!

OKAY! SEE YOU LATER, BLACKIE!

MRAR?

SHE FELL ASLEEP?

ZZZ

SHE MUST HAVE WORN HERSELF OUT.

WELCOME HOME, CHI.

MYA~

HEH...

NRR...?

74

The end

Chi Feels Lonely, Part 1

76

Continued in Part 2

Chi Feels Lonely, Part 2

OH, WHATEVER...

DADDY!! LET'S PLAY!

MYAA!!

...

SHMP

WHAT'S WRONG WITH EVEWYONE?!

BT AM

HUH...?

MYAAA!!

EVEWYONE!!

PLAY WITH CHI!!

MYAMYAA!!

MYA!

MOMMY, LET'S PLAY~!! HERE!

WHAP

HUUUUUSSH...

IT'S SO QUIET...

...

OH, CHI. YOU PICKED UP THE TRASH FOR ME? THANKS.

HUH...?!

TOSS

IT'S WEIRD...

MYAA~

77

Continued in Part 3

78

Continued in Part 4

Chi Feels Lonely, Part 4

Continued in Part 5

Chi Feels Lonely, Part 5

Continued in Part 6

Chi Feels Lonely, Part 6

IT WAS FUN HANGING OUT, COCCHI~

MYA

KEH, I GUESS.

MRAR

HEEY!!

MYAA!!

YOUR HOUSE IS OVER THERE, RIGHT?

YEAH!

MYA MYA~!!

EVEWYONE!

SEE YA!

BYE-BYE!

HUUUSSH

CHI'S HOME!

MYAA!

HUH? IT'S DARK...

MYAAN...

Continued in Part 7

Chi Feels Lonely, Part 7

The end

Chi Thinks of Home, Part 1

HAA, THAT WAS YUMMY.

MYA

WUFF!!

TIP TIP TIP

CHI...

LOVE, SHAKE.

WUFF ♪

SQEEZ

SQEEZ

SO THIS IS HIS HOME.

WUFF WUFF WUFF

Good doggie. Love.

LOOKS LIKE FUN.

THIS IS TOO SMALL...

WE'RE SO COZY AND WARM, AREN'T WE?

WUFF

HOME SEEMS LIKE A NICE PLACE.

...

WUFF ♪

MRR

COCCHI, YOU'VE GOT A NICE HOME, TOO.

KEH! THIS AIN'T A HOME.

Continued in Part 2

Chi Thinks of Home, Part 2

Continued in Part 3

Chi Thinks of Home, Part 3

Continued in Part 4

MYAAA~!

MYAA!! MYAAA!!

MYA...!!

CHI, WHAT'S WRONG? ARE YOU HUNGRY?

MAYBE...

MYA...!!

ARE YOU THIRSTY?

MYAAA~!

MYAA!!

MYAAN!

IT LOOKS LIKE CHI IS TRYING TO TELL US SOME-THING.

CHI...?

MYAAN!

Continued in Part 5

87

Continued in Part 6

Chi Thinks of Home, Part 6

Continued in Part 7

Chi Thinks of Home, Part 7

BY THE WAY, WHAT WERE YOU FIGHTING ABOUT?

OH... ACTU-ALLY...

WHAT IS THIS?!

HUMANS SOMETIMES DO THINGS LIKE THIS...

MRAR?!

MRR...

IT WAS THIS...

I WANTED TO MAKE THIS THE ALBUM'S FIRST PAGE.

OKAY, WE'RE READY!!

3...

2...

1...

SWOOSH

WHAT ARE YOU SAYING?! THIS ONE IS BETTER!

YEAH, BUT...

CHRP CHRP

IT'S PWEY!

MYA!!

MRAR!!

NRR!!

THEN HOW ABOUT WE TAKE A BETTER PICTURE RIGHT NOW?!

OH, RIGHT!

KSHAK

The end

Chi
When I first saw Chi, I thought, "What a cutie!"
I adored her, but once I found out she was sort of
a troublemaker and had a clever side to her,
I liked her even more.

Blackie
He looks scary, but he's good at looking
after others, so I like him.
I tend to draw him with a longer face.

Cocchi
I like characters that pretend to be aloof but
are really sweet, so I'm very fond of Cocchi.
Cocchi's eyes are surprisingly big, which
I like, too.

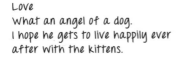

Love
What an angel of a dog.
I hope he gets to live happily ever
after with the kittens.

Konami Kanata

I'm just pulled in by Natsume Kinoko's
energetic version of Chi's world.
There are so many great things about it...
It makes me remember that
Chi is chock full of fun.

Natsume Kinoko

Hello!!
Thank you so much for reading this manga!
It was such a great experience being
involved with a work like
Chi's Sweet Home.

Chi's Sweet Adventures 4

Translation - Jan Cash
Production - Grace Lu
             Anthony Quintessenza

Translation provided by Vertical Comics, 2019
Published by Kodansha USA Publishing, LLC, New York

Originally published in Japanese as *Kyou no Koneko no Chi 4* by Kodansha, Ltd., 2018

This is a work of fiction.

ISBN: 978-1-947194-75-5

Manufactured in Canada

First Edition

Second Printing

Kodansha USA Publishing, LLC
451 Park Avenue South
7th Floor
New York, NY 10016
www.kodansha.us

Vertical books are distributed through Penguin-Random House Publisher Services.

Chi returns to the US in a coloring book featuring dozens of cute and furry illustrations from award-winning cartoonist Konami Kanata.

On Sale Now!

FUKU FUKU

Kitten Tales

Konami Kanata

Craving More Cute Cat Comics?

Want to see more furry feline antics? A new series by Konami Kanata, author of the beloved *Chi's Sweet Home* series, tells the story of a tiny kitten named FukuFuku who lives with a kindly old lady. Each day brings something new to learn, the change of the seasons leads to exciting discoveries and even new objects to shred with freshly-grown claws.

Join FukuFuku and her charming owner on this quietly heartwarming journey of kittenhood.

Both Parts 1 and 2 On Sale Now!